Sonny

Mary Burg

er Sonny

For Jody,
The only real
rock star.
★
7/07/05 !

LEON WORKS

Portions of this work previously appeared in
*Technologies of Measure: A Celebration of
Bay Area Women Writers* and *Boog City*.

Thanks to all who contributed to the realization
of this work, through brilliant critique, friendship,
and tireless support. Especially: Mei-mei Berssenbrugge,
Aja Couchois Duncan, Anne Waldman, Alex Cory,
Beth Murray, Lauren Gudath, Marjorie Bryer,
Rod Golden, Jody Bleyle, Jeff Clark,
Rachel Bernstein, and Renee Gladman.

Designed and composed by Quemadura
Leon Works logo by Caitlin Parker
Printed on acid-free, recycled paper

LEON WORKS: New York

For the ones who have the same parents as me

Note on the Refrigerator

Only keep in mind that I've never wanted to underestimate
the high-scoring malfeasance of your particular spread
of doting uncles, splayed, as they were, in formation,
like barnacles nursing the roof of a well-tended mouth.

ANN VERONICA SIMON

[1968–2003]

This is why we will have to accept the fact that
no one of us really will ever know very much.
This is why we shall have to find comfort in the
fact that, taken together, we know more and more.

J. ROBERT OPPENHEIMER

[1904–1967]

Sonny

This boy raised rabbits and kept them in cardboard pens in the yard.

He showed the rabbits at the fair. He sold the rabbits for pets, or for fur, or for food.

―――――――――――

Once when it snowed very hard the boy had to climb on the roof of the house and push the snow off with a broom.

His sisters looked out through the glass front door.

―――――――――――

What this boy liked best about representation was the way it consoled him for being alive.

What this boy liked best about being alive was the way it consoled him for the immateriality of representation.

1

But this was something new—
something out of all proportion—

Once it was dangerous to know that you were not the center. Then the knowledge put us at the center once again. What other creature knew the world that way? We outlasted our own credibility.

We broke our world apart and started over, broke it and rebuilt it in a different form. Now we were teaching nature to remake itself. An abstract version of a civic form. If there was no creation or destruction, what we valued was what we used to build the form.

We looked for one event that would begin or end, a single mark that everything was organized around.

The climax turning unextraordinary when it repeats. So the haze of arousal, undistinguished, punctuated repeatedly

blue, gray, orange.

It was the moment of implosion that we lived for but the aftermath that made it interesting.

———————————

They mean so many things when they say "brother." Almost always they mean more than a picture on the wall.

This one was natural, made with an element in nature.

———————————

Because it isn't possible to explain what we did in terms of knowing, if we didn't know but thought we did, believing that we did,

in order to do anything it's necessary to separate one thing from the others, one thread pulled through the air, to understand is different from the thought,

the rabbit freezes, twitches, cocks its ears, eyes blinking— to act is different from the understanding of the act— the rabbit tenses, springs, and disappears,

the act is over and the thought remains—
bouncing across the field and vanishing,

we fell back on the only thing we knew.
Skinning rabbits for fur or for food.

It was the aftermath of industry, when industry had spent
itself and moved away, delivered too well on its promises,
and had to take them back. The problem was, we gave them
more, and they expected more again, they wanted things
and time to use their things.

We forced the needle up and then we couldn't keep it there.

Hunting knife drawn down an exposed belly, a beaded line
of blood before it's pulled apart, the anatomical candor, not
animal, not meat,

it was a natural thing but one we'd never seen before.

———————————

What this boy did best was what could not be used for anything.

Through every stage of history, we try to find the thing we recognize.

What this boy liked best,
the end of everything, over and over again.

In the aftermath we see a clean trajectory, a feat that we can easily repeat. Simple, like a gun. A bullet through a barrel through a head.

Of course we don't have many relics from that first time—a little twisted rebar from the tower. We know we'll never find the hull rusting on the ocean floor.

That's why the picture is significant.

We fought the only way that we were able to—we calculated things the world had never known. We carved pieces of a puzzle we made up as we went on. We knew what we were after—or we knew what we were starting from. It's hard to realize now that we were so unsure—

This girl believed her secret boyhood was an arrow, sharp and slender, that would pierce the black smoke around her head and reach clear sky.

This girl believed the small civilizations she invented would be apparent to anyone. This girl held as if in one hand the nexus of a solitary game in the driveway one afternoon, a mother's borrowed dress that hung down to her ankles and her bare feet, and a change in herself with the loose folds around her legs, a sense that she was not walking anymore, she was no longer a person making her way in the world, she was waiting.

She believed the smallest worlds she invented pulsed like blood cells through anyone's veins. Her worlds bumped and clustered and streamed. They were transparent and filled with tiny internal structures—nebulae and networks— each more detailed than the whole. She lay down and felt the worlds settle inside her as if she were a sack of dry beans. When she opened the sack the worlds poured out in a pile in her hands.

———————————

When this girl's neighbor caught baby rabbits—flushed shrieking from their warren as he stood startled among his tomatoes, holding the garden hose—the girl took the rabbits and put them in a cardboard box in the yard. She fed them milk with a plastic doll's bottle, which they demolished with their sharp teeth.

The girl posed for pictures of the rabbits with her friend. When some of the rabbits got away, and some of them died, the girl and her friend and her friend's dad took the last rabbit to a farm and set it free.

————————

What is individual about this girl is what is not visible. What is visible is what is not individual—it is what she has acquired through mimicry and recapitulation. It is what the others also know.

————————

This boy married his wife after stopping to help her and her friend stranded with a flat tire by the side of the road.

He worked in a meat-packing plant until he retired.

Now they have a motor home, a summer home, a winter home, two dogs, three sons, and three daughters-in-law.

He was riding a motorcycle when he met her.

His mother died, and he was raised by another, younger mother, someone else's mother.

He got the name because he was his father's oldest son.

When he was sixty-five, he announced that he did not like the name.

For his first communion, he wore a white shirt, white knickers, white stockings, white shoes, and clutched a white bible and rosary.

In the army, he allowed them to call him John, though none of his names was John.

When he met his wife, he told her that his name was John.

When his wife went traveling, he went to visit his sons, first one and then the other. Each one asked him to spend the night, but he declined; he couldn't leave the dogs alone, and he couldn't bring them to stay with his sons.

His third son, also named John, lived too far away for a day's drive.

———————————

The real atom is more complicated. The nucleus is not a sun; still less are the electrons planets.

It was enough to consider every system as an assembly of smaller ones, with entities that could be represented as weights or spheres.

The future of a particle could only be expressed in terms of probability.

———————————

Because it wasn't possible for anyone. Our heroes marked, slight flaws that might be covered up in photographs but that we would always know were there.

Everything we read or heard or saw reminded us they weren't like us—if they walked in through our doors they wouldn't recognize the drinks we offered them.

At that time, when we were good, there was one way to win; the symmetry of working toward one thing gave us identity that only clarified with time.

If in the moment we were clouded with anxiety, it would be hard later to believe that there had ever been a doubt. Few could be persuaded later of the infinite detail, the myriad near-misses, discouragements and flaws and outright blunders.

———————————

What they wore that day or how their faces did or didn't look alike.

A grandmother's grandmother's gray eyes faded almost to transparency, leaning over with the weight of her own head. A crocheted shawl, a dress with perfect stitches she had hand-sewn even when her eyes had started to fail.

The baby waves, unblinking and amazed. His tiny, spotless shoes.

Young man perched on the arm of the daybed, his thin hair damp and combed but still not smooth, white shirt with bony wrists protruding, tie arduously arranged, only his boots looked comfortable, stained with warm milk sloshing from a metal pail, the green of hay.

Her eyes fixed on what was not in front of her, she knew the child's astonishment even as she slipped farther from her own, head tilted toward what had slipped away;

what could come close to what she didn't say, when they misplaced even her name, a shawl made in a country left behind, and now they were from here instead of there;

something had not been right when they were there, something had made somebody think it would be better to be here,

this was their heirloom, that some of them at least had come because they wanted to,

seeing what no one remembered,

leaf-pattern draperies that concealed a closet or a hall, a wall hung with winter coats showing between the gap.

11

The feet of what they called the Virgin Mary rising past the picture frame surrounded by a ring of saints; a man with a shepherd's staff holding what first looked like a lamb but then revealed itself to be a baby boy.

Because the wind doesn't blow all the time, it can't supply all of our needs.

I am shown the picture and told, "This is your brother." Thick dark hair, brown eyes, a smooth jaw—nothing in the picture contradicts what I am told.

He rode at night, with a chocolate bar and a canteen.

As if family began with automobile, motorcycle, sports car, sedan.

His thick pomaded hair.

From the tree house above the creek onto the rocks—

This boy's hero was a terrorist.

The man rose from his chair, shouting—

A walk through dry leaves to the intersection with two gas stations, across four lanes of traffic then three more to a place that was neither home nor school.

The girl ate the chocolate, six-ounce ingots in white wrappers with a coarse-screened photo of her school, a banner declaring "World's Finest."

There is your brother.

This girl made stories out of artifacts. She made up memories and the people that they happened to. This girl knew family was a wall of photographs, people who looked a little bit like her.

When the neighbor lady answered the door, a bloodstained handkerchief held to her nose.

This boy repeated himself when he got drunk. After various family members howled for him to stop, he muttered the same words over and over more quietly to himself.

She kicked through the dry leaves. She felt the headache that came from too much chocolate.

A boy who had the same parents as me.

———————

The face betrays a caginess, an inability to account for itself, for the last twenty-five years of itself.

Embarrassment at having a past, at being subject to scrutiny even in his absence.

———————

For some, occasional tears from the children when the father comes home drunk or not at all, but dried quickly by

the next day, when all pile into the car for a trip to the water slide and then ice cream.

This boy made a simple burglar alarm with his electronics
set. The wires ran conspicuously along the windowsill.
"They're supposed to show," he said. "When somebody cuts
the wires is when the alarm goes off."

Even if the succeeding generation abhorred his politics,
they shared the belief that a truth could be forced from
poetry.

———————————

From the photograph one could almost believe they were
the kind of family one had lived next door to, with the kind
of children one's children had fought with, the kind of dog
one had chased from one's yard.

She learned to pluck the thick tomato worms, miniature
monsters rearing back in their delicate, soft ferocity.

An accordion in the attic.

The attic grows large, the things in it farther apart. Instead of going downstairs one goes farther away.

———————————

There were the men, working feverishly in a secluded but elaborate makeshift lab. They were excited. They were stimulated. They believed that what they did could change the world. There were their wives. The wives wore clothes that were too nice for makeshift desert towns.

Fire in the fireplace, a brick house anyone would love. Legs curled on the sofa while the sun sank out of sight.

He said to the officer, "These affairs are hard on the heart."

———————————

This mother, years before she was a mother, rode a train through prairies in the middle of her country, to a town ten times as big and seven hundred miles farther than the biggest place she'd ever been.

She went to take care of the boy with no mother, the oldest son of the oldest son, she was sixteen, she knew how to act like a mother, her brother—now a father, still his father's oldest son—took her out to meet young people, handsome boys and laughing girls, evenings at the lakeside, dancing, drinking, winning prizes in the midway games, shrieking on the roller coaster ride.

The brother got another wife, another mother to his oldest son and then a daughter and then another; his sister, still not a mother, moved in with another brother, with his wife who wouldn't be a mother.

Carnivals turned into waitress shifts, straight-seamed stockings and sensible heels, a cook who came to know her by the sound of her walk.

How this sister turned into a mother.

A bride at nineteen, a mother at twenty. And again and again.

They built a house, a small square framed in yellow brick, it was the war, a house could be no larger than the government allowed, it was small but it was new, they planted maple trees and cherry trees and apple trees and grapes.

The house was on the quiet street. Her first boy kept rabbits outside in the yard.

She walked to church—across a quiet street and then a busy street—less than a block away. She saw the sacred heart, blood pouring through his hands.

Again. And again. And again.

———————

Oppenheimer enjoyed his new title, Coordinator of Rapid Rupture.

That women enact a form of attention—toward the work of art or the male artist—that the photograph posits as paradigmatic.

———————

Their dream for an unmediated transfer from intention to matter *was* the subject matter.

A response that acknowledged pointlessness by making a subject out of it.

And then without a sound, the sun was shining. The sand hills at the edge of the desert were shimmering in an almost colorless light. The object like a small sun on the horizon was still too bright to look at. After another ten seconds or so it dimmed into something more like a huge oil fire, shaped a little like a strawberry. It rose from the ground, but remained connected by a stem of swirling dust. I thought of a red-hot elephant standing on its trunk.

The boy rode his horse through the canyon with bread and a canteen of water. He took a bridle but no saddle. His parents, only fifty and already old, were asleep and didn't hear him leave.

Summer-brown shoulder blades bent backward over the rocks under the trees. The body bounced as if it didn't know it was alive.

He worked as a bowling pin spotter on weekday evenings and bided his time to run away.

A family made of photographs.

––––––––––––

The mother knew her oldest boy liked elephants. When he left home she saved his favorite elephant. She gave it back to him before she died.

A wall of photographs, a cache of memories. It was as personal as history, as personal as strangers standing in the yard.

––––––––––––

The president walked over to the Russian leader and casually remarked that the United States had just tested a new and powerful weapon. The Russian said he was glad to hear it and said he hoped America would make "good use of it against the Japanese." After this awkward exchange, the president withdrew.

Out west, the general was confident that the little boy would be as powerful as the fat man.

––––––––––––

As Breslow drove east on Highway 380, he discovered that he'd left his respirator back at the L-7 position. Ahead of him lay a valley covered with a stratum of sandlike radioactive dust. Closing the windows, he drove into it while breathing through a slice of bread. As the smoke pots had indicated, the radioactive cloud sank into the nearby valleys.

Much to their dismay, the team discovered a family living less than a mile from there. It consisted of Mr. and Mrs. Raitliffe, both of whom were over fifty, and their ten-year-old son. The house was not registered on any of the monitors' maps, and no one knew it was there.

The elder Raitliffes had slept through the detonation, and the boy had ridden his horse to Bingham early that morning. Since he did not return until late that night, he probably missed most of the heavy exposure that fell on Hot Canyon. Everyone appeared healthy except Mr. Raitliffe, who complained of "nervousness, tightness in the chest, and poor teeth." These symptoms had bothered him for years.

———————————

The man rose from his chair.

Rooting through thirty-five or fifty years of history.

14 July 17:00 hours. Gadget complete. Should we have the chaplain here.

A fanatic is a fanatic is a fanatic.

Oppenheimer stood in the control room doorway, where he kept an eye on the sky and weather but also watched over the workers in the shelter. To those around him he seemed torn between fear that the bomb would fail and fear that the shattering plan would work. He turned to an officer next to him and said, "Lord, these affairs are hard on the heart."

Suddenly, Oppenheimer halted in midstride. His head was cocked like a dog scenting game. He turned and stalked back to an office.

Inside, a man sat slumped on a straight-backed wooden chair, staring fixedly at a blackboard. He was unshaven and disheveled.

Yellow brick of the new house already old, the children old, the photographs old.

The electric fence at the end of the road. A tree house down by the stream.

This girl's first bicycle a heavy, rusted cruiser left behind by someone in a photograph. She rode standing on the pedals, too small to reach the seat.

A boy who had the same parents as me.

I watched the rabbit watch me kill it.

It blasted; it pounced; it bored its way through you. It was a vision that was seen with more than the eye.

Oppenheimer stood silently behind the man. Together they stared at the jumble of equations.

The cat's water bowl reflecting on the ceiling.

It was seen to last forever.

A fanatic.

For some the unhappiness is for the youngest member gone astray—not smiling, not talking at dinner; eventually, not sleeping in the family house or in any house, not bathing, not living the way other people live, coming home every so often to ask, "Can I have some money? Can you do something for me?"

The broad terra cotta windowsills that collected the fine red dust. The heavy aluminum blinds with frayed webbing, as old as the windows they hung from. More closets than one person could be expected to fill. The sun streaming down the flat, straight, endless alleyways. An irregular cadre boring through the dumpsters each day.

What at first appeared to be a man revealed itself, on closer approach, as a cloud of black flies, hovering in a column solid but indistinct, in fact not so different from a man but with more space between the particles.

———————

This girl's mother was a mother long before the girl was born. The mother of one and another was born, the mother of others and others were born.

The crossroads—church-home-school-work—that occupied all of her household all of the time, all within the same two blocks.

Eating concrete to get out of the house.

———————

There was a feeling of mountain resort mixed with army camp.

It would be well that the world knew about the possibility, rather than it being something that was kept secret. We all decided that that was right, and that we ought to go back into the laboratory and work as hard as we could.

I didn't want for it to be dangerous. There was a chance that it would be—could be—very dangerous.

———————————

The present's vacancy meant that the past rushed into the vacuum; and if the past, in its own present, had been vacant too, it took on materiality in being telescoped, in being made a specimen and examined from the outside.

A boy who had the same parents wrote, "Happy Easter!

I haven't seen you since the funeral."

———————————

In vain she struggled against the weight of accumulated concrete. Pinned as if by an earthquake.

They transformed artistic production from the conveyance of stable symbolic values into a game of potential meaning.

To accept the liberating, if dangerous, potential of epistemological uncertainty.

If the boy who rode with his back to the blast, if he had the same parents as me—no, exactly the same, soft teeth and hard bones. If he rode away from what he didn't know about, if he vanished into air.

———————

Blue eye shadow swabbed tentatively onto this girl's lids.

Curled photographs of the rabbits
in cardboard pens in the yard.

This boy in photographs. Three bicycles posed with the children.

We were lying there, very tense in the early dawn.

This boy pounded the carbon cores of flashlight batteries with a hammer in the basement. It went on for several days until his mother learned it was for making gunpowder.

This boy was like his father in name only.

The sudden revolution in consciousness that he had hoped for but had not really expected had not come to pass.

Three bicycles posed with the children that day.

We believed—for who wouldn't, facing the limits of knowledge.

The way the mother's talents visited themselves on the children, a knack for sewing, a way with gadgets, skill at balancing a checkbook.

She taught them blood welling from the sacred heart, pooling through warm fingers, staining the fleece of the lamb.

The man rose from his chair, shouting, "I've been looking for that mistake for two days!"

Their games, their plots, their ambitions worn externally, in complete absence of shame.

The boy who watched his father urinating on a rock, who closed his eyes and believed his chaos was a woman he would struggle with but never tame, this boy who nearly strangled being born, who made his mark—a drip, a splatter—like the paint would trap his battle with his woman-side, this boy created chaos that the others could consume. The transfer of his inner battle to the outside through his hands became the hero's tale. This boy who rarely spoke swallowed his city, country, history, and name.

The boy who rarely spoke wrote when his father died, "It is of the utmost difficulty that I am able to write, and then only miles from my want and feeling."

———————————

Three children on their bicycles pose for a moment they don't understand, for one who takes their picture, who will leave the town, the parents, and the yard.

The boy who raised the rabbits has already left the town, the parents, and the yard—if they believed a war could drive them from each other's arms, it was a war that was invisible.

It was a father who believed to keep a balance in the bank meant that he loved his family.

And those children on their bicycles, who watched the grown-up children leave and leave and leave.

———————————

This girl ran races with herself, around the outside of the house, sometimes her big self won, sometimes her small.

She pressed her back against the locked back door and pulled the screen door hard against her; the German shepherd barked and barked a few feet from her face; later the mother said, "He was only trying to keep you safe."

———————————

In one of the boy's favorite books, a young elephant doesn't fit in with the others because he doesn't like to take baths in the river.

One day, an explorer from a faraway place, wearing a pith helmet and an implausible beard, appears and offers to take the elephant away to the circus and make him a four-star stupendous success.

Various things happen. The explorer gives the elephant a bath, and the elephant likes the bath. But once he is clean, the elephant looks ordinary and not so impressive. The explorer finds another, bigger elephant to take to the circus, and the first elephant stays behind and learns to love taking baths in the river. He is so content, he grows very large and even more impressive than before. The explorer returns eventually and makes another offer—to make the first elephant a five-star stupendous success. The elephant declines.

"I am so happy here with my friends, in the lovely river, that I could never, never leave. I can not go."

The story is called *The Elephant's Dilemma*.

The elephant's first bath, given him by the explorer, is in a giant red wooden tub. Water to fill the tub is carried by native helpers in large jars on their heads.

The teacher asked the boy to tell the class about the historic attraction he had visited, that was depicted in the class's history book.

"Does it look like the picture?" the teacher asked.
The boy pondered. "It's not that clean," he finally declared.

Two days later, the man said, "Well, I am most disappointed. I am very tired of scrubbing, besides it is useless. You have shrunk so much that you could never be a success. As the most STUPENDOUS, SUPER–SUPER, COLOSSAL——you are impossible."

And he was. Anyone could see that he was.

This girl stood in the driveway where the boy had stood, to each of them the drive was empty. For each of them the other wasn't there, for him she came too late, for her he wasn't there at all.

Leaving meant that nothing ever changed again, that everyone became themselves, unchanging, in revolving scenes.

The man who kept a balance in the bank.
The man who worked and went to church and read the
    evening paper.
The man who grew up farming, ran a dairy, restaurant, bar,
    and trailer park.
The man who bought American family cars and pickup
    trucks.
The man who owned a house, one house and then another
    for his growing family, from the time his oldest son was
    three.
The man who smoked a pipe, then gave it up.
The man who liked to have a beer.

The man who almost lost his leg, who almost lost his ear.

The priest who told the woman, "Pray for guidance, pray to
    bear your lot in life."
The priest who told her, "God has chosen what you are
    to be."

33

The man who thrived for fifty years on work he learned at twenty served his country in the war in a munitions factory and burned his lip at break time drinking coffee from a mason jar.

As fallout rained down on the milk cows, as Strontium-90 was pronounced on the radio and overheard in grocery stores.

This man kept a balance in the bank.

As his offspring grew from four to seven, as his wife grew more babies for more than twenty years, as his children stayed alive through bouts of hemophilia, drunk driving, chemotherapy, attempted suicide, he made it to his grave with a shattered shin and a mangled heart.

This man before he was a man, with thick round glasses and a woolen hat, with sleeves too short and bony wrists, self-conscious and alone before the lens, facing forward, looking to the side, his mouth could be a smile or a scowl.

To rely on memory decades before memory began.

The early place looks like the better place simply because it's done.

———————————

We didn't know we were at war until we found ourselves in pieces.

Each one peeling off, ray from a Catherine wheel.

The one who took the picture went away.

———————————

The boy twenty-five years before me. He had the same parents as me. He had two little sisters and then he had three. He had two little brothers and then he had me. He liked rabbits and cameras and elephants and cars. He looked a little bit like me.

———————————

Who tried to kill herself but couldn't die.

Who packed her clothes and waited for the train.

Who in the city bought bamboo birdcages, batik scarves, and leather furniture. Who hung shades and heavy drapes to block the sun.

Who went to operas, ballets, art museums. Who bought books and magazines. Who had a job. Who rode the bus. Who ate alone.

Who took photographs, who was nobody's mother.

Who took photographs that showed the children short or fat or thin.

––––––––––

Each child had a bicycle. The girl's was gold, with training wheels.

The knowledge she acquired was of use to her.

She could not tell anyone.

What she knew was not in order.

What she said was out of order.

The way things happened was in any order.

They had had a swing but now only the metal frame was left.

They had had a dog but now only his picture and his name were left. Blackie.

She tried to hear the people calling from across the gap. She recognized them from a distance, but not up close.

The atomic cattle, like the atomic cat, grew small white stars where the fallout rained on them.

When this boy rode his horse away, he rode away from everything that hadn't happened yet.

His parents slept through the bomb.

This boy dreamt of being a poet, architect, or scientist.

This boy knew when he had done wrong it could not be undone.

Desert—canyon—mountain range. A boy who knew the West as a vacation. A boy who knew nothing else.

The boy who threaded his horse through canyons.

As stone heads and wooden masks stood in for the terror they made themselves.

They made themselves.

Who would declare,

I am become Death.
I am nine times brighter than the sun.
I eat the air.

———————————

Adhesive tape, the last thing added to the bomb.

———————————

His rented suit, his sculpted hair, his shiny shoes, the ring a new addition to his suntanned hand.

The children who would start as varying composites of him and her, their bright dark eyes, their shiny hair, their brilliant faces, complicated minds.

They fought their mother. Before they could reason, argue, or run away. It was they who taught her that she had a will: to mold their willfulness, to shape what they would be.

That the girls be sexually immaculate, the boys free of effeminacy.

His sculpted hair, his pleated trousers, a smile that struggled across his sullen face.

To have a *handsome* family, girls well married, boys respectably employed, to drive to church each Sunday.

This girl sitting in the closet with a plastic rosary, glowing luminescent in the dark. A toy sent from the missionary, *Thank you for your generous donation*.

School clothes and Christmas toys from Sears.

The mother's bunions from poor-fitting shoes.

Not this girl's red patent leather lace-ups with the clunky heels, the lime green sneakers for gym day, ears pierced in sixth grade, spoon rings, mood rings, apple core necklaces, glitter t-shirt appliqués.

———————————

A girl who pasted pictures of her brother on the wall.

New couple in the back seat of the limousine.

See his thick hair. See his handsome, moody smile. See how uncomfortable he is. See how he thinks about leaving.

Sitting idly on a swing. A girl who taught herself to climb to the top of the swing set, grabbing the A-frame side poles, shinnying up hand by hand, throwing one leg over the top and twisting up to sit astride.

The tops of the hedges were dusty with lack of rain.

A girl who saw the back windows of the house——now at eye level instead of over her head; a girl who saw things but was no nearer to them.

Riding on the bus. Some got on early, some left late. Some chatted with the one beside them, some were silent. Some rode for miles never knowing who the other was or what right or cause they had to be there.

Dark blue rose-patterned carpet. Years of Christmas in the living room. The size of the children, the toys they held, and some of the furniture changing over time.

Smiling in a black straw hat. A dandelion in one chubby hand. Tilting like she wasn't used to walking yet.

Lines around the baby mouth you almost recognize.

There is your mother.

Uncle standing in a rowboat in the sun.

41

Uncle a security guard at Timken Steel.

Uncle mowed his lawn diagonally—southwest to northeast one week, southeast to northwest the next.

Uncle nursed his second wife, helped her bathe and dress and eat. Uncle shaved and put on aftershave. After his wife died the second time he cooked his meals and every week his youngest daughter visited. She had been a nun and now she had a boyfriend. She had been a majorette and now she laughed out loud. She called her brother by the name he'd had in childhood.

———————

A sagging cabinet for storing toys. This girl piled toys on top and sat inside.

Chairs stacked in rows against the restaurant wall. She built a train and climbed amid the upturned legs.

Later when she fell out of the tree, she said, "I had a dream."

Body bouncing on the rocks under the trees.

We didn't know the language and we didn't know that they were speaking. We earned our passage slowly and our right of entry slower still. We had a point of reference, unfixed but findable, spines pressed together notch to notch, *still point in the turning world.*

If nothing is allowed but these pastel figures, these wax forms, is that to say there is nothing else, or that what is there allows us to see this? Why does it matter, that we can see these forms? If these forms had not been made, would we still know how to see them?

What kind of world demands that we should see what's there or what is possible?

A grandfather's grandfather walked across the country, had some sons and daughters, cut down trees.

The vocabulary words we learned—*family*, *brother*, *home*. A brother is a boy who has the same parents as you. A boy who eats dinner with you. In a house with your parents, the parents who belong to both of you. You look alike, the two of you. In school, the teachers and the other children know you are the same. You have the same family. You have the same name.

Even the ones who lived right through it didn't know what they were witnessing.

———————

A quiet conversation murmured intermittently.

People learning to be people. Talking, sitting, crying.

How was it supposed to work out, raising the young and having a society?

———————

This boy who would be almost silent. Holding pictures of his recent cars. His swimming pool. Pink mini dress and long legs stretched out on his pool table. "She's not my girl-friend," is his explanation.

Who vacuumed spent matches from the carpet. Warehouse windows looking out across the roofs as far as she could see. Small towns disintegrated in the brick of her new city.

In the canyon where the boy went riding there was no one else. His horse knew the way because they went the same way every time. The horse was scared of nothing except snakes and mountain lions. The boy was scared of nothing except getting caught.

Each man trained hard and matched his skills against the other men. Each man believed that he could be the hero.

Starting barroom brawls, taking a plane off base unautho-rized—even boasting of the mission secrets to civilians—all were tolerated if the man was good enough.

The man they chose to fly the mission knew before the others knew. He kept training with the others as if anyone might go. Not even he knew all the details—only that it would be dangerous in a different way than anything they'd ever done before. Using a weapon that no one had invented yet.

It was important that several be ready, in case something went wrong or in case they decided on a second mission or a third.

————————————

This man who ran a dairy, who bought farmers' milk and bottled it and carried it to people's doors, who bought some paneled trucks and hired men to carry milk to people's doors. He liked this modest girl who wanted babies, went to church devotedly, and looked at him with expectation in her eyes.

It was exciting for a girl not quite nineteen. She felt she had to please her husband and felt happy when she did.

————————————

Children growing up and changing everything—their healthy bodies, chanting, *Can't you see the blood of Birming-*

46

ham-Saigon-Kent State-the Palestinians-the Nicaraguans on this country's hands?

———————

It was completed with white X's of adhesive tape. It was assembled in a tent—a circus freak, a sinner come to the revival.

The same tape used for heavy bandages. The surface of the metal sphere pockmarked, irregular—a little moon with wires sticking out. As venerated as the source of life.

Such preciousness—the thing existed for a day.

———————

Men in khakis and short sleeves who leaned in, examining. Men with glasses and neat hair, who had their lives ahead of them, who'd left their lives behind, who'd brought their wives along. Wives who had their hair done in the nearest town and ruined new high heels on rocky roads. Wives who lived for cocktails and the evening radio.

47

Men who stayed up all night, chalking equations, arguing, their ties thrown off, inhaling cigarettes.

The chalk as fascinating as the gin.

———————————

"I didn't want it to be dangerous."

There were children born—twenty-seven in four years. There were divorces, infidelities, six deaths.

———————————

A way to make this one thing happen, pull it out and put it in a set of steps a man could understand—

then rivers could be harnessed into turning turbines night and day, factories for food and cars and airplanes could grow clusters of cities on the desert floor.

———————————

This boy who wasn't there took up more room than anyone who was. His mouth a thin set line, this boy whom they set

48

store by, who liked elephants, who stood in his new snow-suit on the wooden porch.

This girl who played with photographs collected dust like it was her experience. It was important to preserve dust in the same arrangement it was found.

———————————

It was his charming, open eyes, his slender face, alacrity with an equation. Angular physique well-suited to the fashions of his day, the wide-legged trousers, fitted coats, the broad lapels—

super models with no figures of their own, suited for the fantasies of other men.

When he moved his god aside to place his own mind at the center of his universe.
Did that make him more a part of nature or more different from?

———————————

The perfect laboratory. Searing heat of inquiry. When had there ever been such intellect, when had there been such urgency?

Knowledge itself could have no obligations. Waiting for its own discovery. Science created circumstances in which knowledge was unveiled.

If it had not occurred to nature to arrange itself in such a way before, did that make the men less natural or more?

It was a knowledge that could not be blamed on Eve.

It was the paradigm for victory. The crucible of knowledge and emergency.

———————

Living room furniture bought with trading stamps—a metal bookshelf, set of TV trays.

This baby boy who went to war and wasn't wounded, who came back and met his wife.

The older ones brought memories in black and white. A tiny girl on roller skates. Sisters in handmade clothes. Watching a brother shovel snow.

A young man left, an old man stayed behind.

Kissing with his cigarette mouth.

Could there be a perfect language that could answer any problem it could pose? Would it be more like math or poetry?

_____

Riding her tricycle into the glass front door—

His was the beauty behind everything. Hips tapered to the disappearing waist, limbs moved by tensile cords and tackles, grace and specificity.

A soaring verticality uninterrupted by dissenting lines. When they began to realize their processes could make something completely new—

who knew the specificity of randomness and anarchy—

_____

It's not a happy ending that we need—
that's why none of the apocalypses will do.

_____

A boy who bought Corvettes and Cadillacs, who wore the kind of clothes that Elvis wore.

It was a cosmology made of scraps that anyone could find, a strand of hair, a picture of a steer.

———————

The tensile strength of his, the perfect beauty. Faceless history of intimate details.

With a power over nature out of all proportion to their strength. Who in their wisdom made their knowledge subject to their will.

———————

A grandmother in a flowered dress, grandfather in the driveway with a baby boy, for years and years the same driveway with different girls and boys. The maple trees taller each time by degrees, measuring the years between the children.

A flowered dress stretched wide by years of children.

With a kitchen garden, chickens, and a cow, it was enough to feed the girls and boys and teach them to do the same. Everyone knew everyone, they went to the only church and sent their children to the only school.

A grandfather's grandfather walked across the state when that was just a name for wild land.

An old man's memory of an old man. A long black beard, forests that fell. The men who made the farms and villages, the churches, houses, courthouses, and schools, women who grew vegetables and gathered eggs.

The crossroads—home-church-work-school—multiplied by cars and telephones—

a grandfather's grandfather's black beard reached to his chest. First there were the forests and then there were the cities.

———————

The children with the newborn calf too small still for the men to tell its sex, the children pleaded for a girl, a little cow could live there and grow old, a little bull would go to slaughter or be sold to make a steer.

Comforts doled out to the cows—air conditioning and showers, concrete floors and milk machines—twice a day on every day men pulled milk from the animals—

the uncle with his overalls who limped on his rheumatic knees, who was a full head shorter than his wife, who smiled shyly, went through surgery for two new knees, titanium, so he could walk upright a few years more, worked every day then went to Switzerland to see the Matterhorn.

———————

The first time she had a baby it was like it wasn't happening.

She was a skinny girl with glasses and an eye patch. She saw double, which caused her to bump into things. To fall out of a tree.

When she was sick her mother brought her records. She'd seen opera on TV; her mother bought her boxed sets when she was too sick to listen to them, could only lie there with them in her hands.

She wrote in mirror image and upside down. Sexually in-experienced, the kind of girl who did boys' homework for them rather than go out on dates. She was a regular, reading her poems and ad-libbing, until the building collapsed.

There were only fourteen people there but I saw what I was looking for, people who were revolutionary, who were merging rock and roll and poetry. People were expecting me to help them with their revolutions. I thought, if I'm going to be a leader, where am I leading people to? Sometimes when everybody seems so happy, I feel like my bones are electricity. I have the night. I have the city. I consider myself lucky.

A first baby, grown up now, it could be almost anyone, it could be someone here.

A tomato garden with tomato worms.

"I have no natural ability, just determination."

Can the articulated self-consciousness of adolescence provide a better device than the mute sensitivity of childhood —adolescence with its cartilage not yet completely hardened into bone, with the libido still new to itself, making mistakes but not yet realizing it will make the same mistakes forever, the freshness of a truly new mistake can make you feel like the whole world's ahead of you, the way repeating a mistake makes you feel like a kid again, in either case you feel you can't go on.

When the I began to experience a resurgence, this I who explained what happened to it, understood its place and what that meant—it was still easier to project emotion onto the deaths of someone else's parents than one's own. Uncomfortable in-laws and acquaintances who stood among the folding chairs,

there was an adolescence and it ended, a short time. I'd like to insist that embarrassment was concentrated in one period, bounded by a beginning and an end.

Six and one half years again.

———————————

An abnormally repulsively good little boy
who studied minerals, who gave a lecture at age twelve,
who waited for the elevator rather than climb a flight of
   stairs,

a memory of embarrassment, or that remembered in embarrassment,
locked naked in an icehouse overnight, tormented by his
cabin mates at summer camp.

The West was where frail Eastern boys were sent to find
their strength.
Horses, mountains, sleeping under stars—
the rugged land could turn a sickly boy into a fighting man.
Brown and tough from weeks outside, a boy returned to
math and chemistry with a new sense of being an American.

———————————

He chose a site to build the gadget, they needed space, seclu-
sion, secrecy. They had a bathtub but no air conditioner.

The molds for the explosive lenses had arrived cracked and
pitted—useless to make the trigger. The team worked
around the clock with dental tools to scrape and patch the
castings. It was their job to make it work.

It was a power that not many could endure.

As soon as they learned the structure of the thing they set out to explore the thing itself.

———————

Canyons, arroyos, desert air all fed the heartiness of city boys.

The cities had been devastated and it was with difficulty that a city of sufficient size was found.

Oppie's wife gave him a good luck charm, a four-leaf clover she had found outside. They worked out a message he would send if things went well: "You can change the sheets."

The one who could have seen the problem, who could have done more to change the course of things, in the end could not be found.

———————

They held their heads a little on one side as he did, coughed slightly and paused significantly between sentences, held hands to their lips when they spoke and made obscure comparisons that were meant to sound profound and sometimes were. They picked up his habit of offering a light whenever anyone took out a pipe or cigarette; could be recognized from far away, darting about like marionettes on invisible strings, tiny gas flames between their fingers.

———————————

A fall on the ice during a late month of pregnancy, walking to church with children in the snow. That one was lost but there were more. It was enough for anyone, getting more beds every year and bigger cars. It was enough, but later there were more.

The way children in other families touched each other, tumbled on the floor, had puppies, kittens, backyard tree houses. It was as alien as history.

He is vacant, this brother. He is a vacancy. So in place of a brother I must put something else.

———————————

He was very angry, pacing up and down, and so I said, "Look I'll bet one month of my salary against ten dollars that this thing will work." He took the bet. But then I went away. I couldn't take it anymore, I went into the desert by myself.

He spent the night with the rest of them, camped at the bottom of the tower armed with flashlights and a machine gun.

They had all been given plates of welder's glass to look through when they viewed the sight. One had brought suntan cream.

At the countdown he suddenly thought the thing would act like lightning and he would be electrocuted by the microphone. At minus one he dropped the mic and screamed as loudly as he could, "Zero!"

Back at Base Camp, between the flash and the shock wave, one man had been running his own test. He'd been clutching scraps of paper and as the shock wave hit he let them go. When he measured how far the pieces traveled, he could calculate the blast—twenty thousand tons of TNT equivalent.

I slapped him on the back and I said, "I won the bet." He couldn't do anything but pull out his billfold and then he turned around and said, "George, I don't have it."

Now they knew they didn't need the Russians to help end the war.

That night as he left the celebrations, he came across one of the young scientists stone cold sober retching into the bushes.

I mean a boy who had the same parents as me. Who bore some resemblance in his childhood photos to those of me. Who could be picked out of a lineup as the boy most nearly resembling me.

The self-knowledge of bare feet on cold stone, the coolness, the mild coarse surface against your skin, the unyielding density, the weight you believe in with the testing. The water whose temperature changes the longer you touch it. How can it be said to end?

I won't tell you anything and then I'll tell you everything.

I don't know anything because there isn't anything to know.

A grandmother's faded flowered dress and cat eye glasses and curled hair were all the children could describe of her, they knew her name, they'd seen her handwriting.

A family stored in photographs, when the prints were lost it was the negatives they handled carefully and passed around, memories they didn't really recognize but told each other dutifully, like they'd been a family in a house one time, like they'd all lived together.

———————————

Young parents just discovering the ways it didn't work to be a family. Each child struggling with its own complexity, unknowable, unloving in some way. The constant revelations —we were immigrants, now we're from here—we were from someplace where they do things differently.

You couldn't buy a bigger car then, all the steel was for the war. They all sat on one seat, the boy forward and the girl behind, the baby on the mother's lap, and father drove. It was decades before car seats and many other ways to save a child's life.

———————————

"For life to go on as we know it, millions of people are going to have to die."

We became used to the way a single day could change the world.

Ceremonial martinis and habitual cigarettes.

He was a radical who became a patriot. He was like a lot of others that way.

———————————

It made a little sun. At first she couldn't look and then she couldn't look away.

A sunset in her hand,
a tranquil sea that balanced on its stem.

Her legs drawn up, surveying sunsets from the couch.
No evening started without two or three. If the sun rose twice, it set at least that many times.

Little suns fell past the horizon to the bottom of the well.

Sweet piney smell of desert juniper.

A girl could go a long way with a man like that.

Twilight on the horizon line, fulcrum between night and day, two pieces, black and gray.

A light so bright it took colors away. The air tasted like tin.

The accidental warriors with slide rules and uncombed hair weren't prepared for what would happen if they got it right.

They solved equations and made models that passed the tests. That was as far as they had ever gone. Used to no one understanding what they did, used to talking only to each other.

She had a car accident and he was kicked by a horse.

"Get up," she told her husband. "The sun is rising in the west."

This valley, ignored by everyone. Even planes move faster when it's in their view, like swallows passing through badlands.

We haven't been here so long that we can't remember anything—on the contrary, everything we see here contradicts what we have learned.

I am not sure what I can tell you about this place. I am not even sure it is a place.

Lizards pose fetchingly until you try to get up close to them.

I am not the first to think of leaving here. All down the rows wives put dinner on the table.

I pulled the screen door tight against me while the German shepherd barked into my face.

She'd needed someone she could make demands on. Someone elegant, ambitious, a man with wherewithal.

Little suns and charming smiles. He could persuade a wolf to let go of a lamb.

In their house on Bathtub Row, a white-painted brick fireplace, a sofa, a few chairs—

an inchworm wrapped in silk.

———————

If the sun rose twice—if the sun rose in the west—it is only so in relation to the witness, who knows the earth goes round and round and always, since the earth began, the same direction. The lesson with the grapefruit, orange, and lime—among children the story is believed before the evidence can be understood. As time goes on the mind may reinforce imagination, or the imagination comes to convince itself.

And so when the sun rose at a place where the ordinary sun was not yet visible—this happened, it does not depend on the imagination, the earth and the second sun were in relation such that the second sun lit up the predawn sky, but what is light, a wavelength perceived by various life forms, were it not for these, what would light be—

There was a time before the second sun, and then there was the second sun.

———————

She smoked cigarettes and had no interest in the role of the director's wife.

And the evidence, a green-glass desert floor.

They wore white paper covers on their shoes, and badges that measured how much they had been exposed each day. But day lasts forever with the second sun.

You may think the second sun is setting but it's grown so large you can't see where it ends or understand the time before it started.

In a short time it will be possible to explain everything, and describe everything, and know how everything has come to be. And when knowledge is complete, the second sun will be used only for good and only when everyone agrees. The day will come, and it is coming soon, when we will understand. It will be as if, when someone said, let there be light, instead there was us.

———————————

Shipping containers replaced suitcases as the thing most likely to explode.

When the dust refused to settle and we realized we would never see again, feeling our way among the upright beams, steel was dust, the floors were dust, we ate the dust and breathed it back out, warmed and moistened by our lungs, the dust refused to settle and we called the new place "here," we didn't realize we had been here all along.

Even the rain did nothing to cool the smoking pit.

It took many years to understand the source of light was not ourselves.

———————————

The ones who went away had names. The parents knew some things about each child and remembered some of them. Some things they had known they let slip away. There was a pile of photographs, some with several children, some with a child alone.

———————————

The first time he went west he fell in love. The second time he split in two.

Raising rabbits because they reproduced so fast.

It was exuberance we could not justify.

Speculations are not satisfying and the certainties are few.

Just the simple evidence that things took place. They got from there to here. They came sometime before the oldest living one was born. A faded gray lets go, pressing the baby tightly to her side.

Everything we missed existed somewhere. Even though it never happened, not to us or anyone.

All the phenomena to fill the empty space.

———————————————

This boy decades before me. He has the same parents as me. If we met casually standing in the grocery line we might discover this. The family dairy. Catholic school. Me too.

We might look more closely. See a similarity. Eyes that look chestnut from a certain angle, olive from another, hair mistakable for black. Skin that tans easily—we might revise the family pedigree to add a little Spanish to the French and Swiss.

After finding this surprising thing in common, we might still stand there. One with a carton of milk, one with cigarettes. Waiting our turn in line. Not sure what to say next.

Does it need more history? She was twenty when the first one was born. She stayed fertile for a generation more.

He was born and then everyone else. Things happened, and he went away.

He was married once, but only for a little while. He left town and didn't come again for twenty years. The only thing he ever talked about was cars.

A tinny radio, *I say a little prayer for you*, the incense-fogged, high-ceilinged Sunday, stiff clothes and shiny shoes, the somber, off-key hymns.

We thought the children learned in fractured bits, no continuity.

An errand to the butcher's, money pressed tightly in one hand.
Sunday afternoon, a treat of Coke and potato chips; a brother who loved Corvettes.

70

In those faded eyes was everything they ever knew and
everything they couldn't own; thick boots. Where did
the money for their passage come from?
For every one that left, at least a hundred stayed behind.

There are some people. There are moments spread out over
time. For some of the moments there are artifacts left behind. Some of the same people appear in different places.
Some of the artifacts, fit together, make a story over time.

The boy who rode his horse through the bomb went silver,
transparent, in the light of the bomb and vanished into the
air of the bomb, while the old parents, soft teeth and hard
bones, the old parents slept through the bomb.

The simplest device used a trigger mechanism that almost
anyone could understand—one ball shot through a barrel
and collided with a bigger ball—it was so simple that no one
expected it to work. There was no test—the first use was
the experiment.

There was only one first time.

When the spigot falls off. Where does all the water go?

This boy wanted army boots and signed up with the National Reserve. Before he bought a Cadillac. Before he wore a white tuxedo jacket in the back seat of a limousine. Before he was the first to leave, before the other children talked about him like he wasn't there, before he wasn't there. He went away for weekends and his mother had more children who would look a little bit like her.

Caught in an afternoon rainstorm—

when we learned to think of things as dangerous—a child runs into the street, a baby's father throws him in the air;

giving quarters to the ice cream man. The song grows tinny, fading block to block.

Three babies played in sun suits while somewhere the sun rose twice.

Who watched her babies playing in the sun.

———————————

Renting houses that were already old.

The couple married and immediately discovered they were incompatible. They stayed together fifty years.

Soft-spoken self-reliance. "We didn't want for it to be dangerous."

To find the still point in a turning world—the thing that was the worst gradually faded and reappeared in black and white.

Their complications were erased and others were inserted. Later even a child could be made to understand.

It was impossible to defend what had come before—each time we told the story it was different.

———————————

There was a boy. Different and maybe the same. In a desert in a canyon in a dream. The light went on behind him, in a supernatural electric storm, the silver light burnt through him, through his t-shirt, through his skin, through the horse's skin, they were transparent, they were air.

———————————

One step brought us into the enormous world whose history has yet to be written.

I recommend a very rudimentary beginning. It would be better to not even try to go beyond what one does so modestly, as if it hung together, like the history of Philadelphia.

An actual rather than a fabricated subject.

I have gone into all this detail to give a sense of the total falsehood. So why do we suppose that what we say and do is neutral, when it is full of consequences for the human race?

———————————

It is possible that we stand on nothing more solid than the remnants of memory, a concrete history of disintegration.

74

If memory leads in circles, are they widening or something more?

The streets were filled with red Corvettes, the obvious was held as almost unattainable, there was satisfaction in that kind of aspiration.

———————————

An ordinary man, did he leave because of what he left behind or what he saw ahead?

The ornate tale of sacrifice that called on all the explanation she had generated on her own.

What they said in greeting, what they called each other in this place, headlights turned on careful rubble, passion proven in geometry.

———————————

This girl's secret boyhood rode on horseback followed by the blast. The blast that turned the daylight silver and turned everything to air. When her secret boyhood ended, this girl got off the horse and walked it home. Her secret boyhood's parents, the same parents as hers, slept through the bomb and didn't know. They slept through her secret boyhood and were waiting for their girl to come back home.

———————————

One day when the sun rose, snowflakes settled on the cattle herd and left stars on their heads, a black cat wore new diamonds in its fur. The ranch wife woke up first and told her husband, "Get up now. The sun is rising where it set."

A green glass desert floor.
Eggs that day were boiled in the shell.
The chickens wouldn't eat.

Houses built of anything. A cocktail with a tiny sun.

A boy rode from a canyon on the morning of the second sun, here where no one knew what should be done.

We made a sun.

———————————

All of the bachelors put on uniforms and went to war.

Or how a girl could go from one dimension into five.
A point, a line, a sphere. Geometric proofs cannot explain
   her flourishing.

The brightest light that anyone had ever seen, it changed
our human scale to know we could disintegrate.

―――――――

She needed makeup she had seen in magazines—a smooth
complexion, lashes long and thick—a few blocks to the cor-
ner, the gas station and the traffic light.

There were other streets but only one way to the store.

―――――――

In this girl's secret boyhood she knew what the men believed and what they trusted in. She knew what they were
scared of and she knew what they would do. If there was a
girl whose secret boyhood rode her horse across the canyon, waiting for the blast to hit her in the back, the clean-
cut men in short-sleeved shirts were heroes who did not
survive the fall.

77

After the win we were exuberant.

———————————

Dressing for the camera, assembling and smiling and hold-ing still. A pose that revealed nothing of their lives together, waiting for the flashbulb to explode.

Who could hurl themselves off rocks when these muscles had never been used except for holding still.

———————————

How the houses slip by sideways, fish-shaped between the pavement and the night.

Front door rushing by, spokes spinning, trees grown up around the door, they prove there was a time before.

Drinking cocktails while the sun sank, rolling at the bottom of the well.

With her legs curled, brick wall painted white, heads rolled at the bottom of the well.

78

Looking at it there, a motley ball with white tape X's, clumsy submarine, something patched together from a brittle sketch, you can get some idea.

We were so young then—ready with our suntan lotion and our sunglasses, camping out and waiting for the dawn, telling stories when we couldn't sleep.

Someone had the idea to spread a truckload of mattresses under the tower to break the fall, in case the cables didn't hold.

Our enemy far away, exaggerated teeth and cartoon eyes. They didn't live like us.

The weather man wasn't telling them what they wanted to hear, so they let him go and someone closer to the core took over. They were worried about drift and dispersal but they had to do it that day anyway—there were too many factors riding on it and almost no one knew what they all were.

We have not eaten dinner together, this brother and I. He is not dead. He is not in prison. He is not angry or insane or hiding from the law. He has a modest life enjoying inexpensive drinks at a few uncelebrated bars in the old section of Las Vegas.

He walked over, straining to appear casual, and gave the news as if it were an afterthought. His rival took the news as if he didn't already know.

To tell the truth we needed someone who could recognize what we left out. He didn't know till later why it didn't come as a surprise. See, the victors don't write history; it happens far too often that they don't know why they won.

Our inauspicious start in a gymnasium. We believed the worst was happening. We thought we were our own best hope, learning to use these tools that only we could understand. That everything depended on our manipulating things we'd only recently identified.

But the work we did—chalk dust, headaches, arguments, the office lights still on at 3 a.m.—once the world knew— no, even before that—we felt it breaking up. Then the resentments and rivalries came to seem insignificant—after all we'd done it. We'd won.

This wife who kept her hair done and her sweaters clean got a share of the best food delivered each week and knew more than she should.

———————————

She was the faded edge of failing family. So faint that she was almost colorless.

This girl's secret boyhood understood the overlapping centers of concentric spheres. The centers swirled around each other. The surfaces glided like years.

This girl made up a boyhood for the boy she never knew, the boy who grew up in the house where she grew up, with the parents she grew up with, with the furniture she knew.

———————————

But rarely were our talents so specifically requested, rarely did we find ourselves hustled up to the front lines amid the broad shoulders and deep chests, outfitted with our own passwords and code names.

To think our very calculations might save lives.

The fictions we perpetuated to maintain our understanding—it was necessary to create diversions to sustain our effort over time.

With each new instrument the universe became more clear to us, more clearly ours. There were even some who believed we would fill in all the empty spaces in the chart we'd drawn up of the history of time.

He wore a striped t-shirt and little bib overalls. He sat upright, looking startled.

There were people. They knew each other. Things happened to them that affected each one differently. They were different afterwards. They did things, some knowingly, some unknowingly. Some things they saw happening and couldn't control. Some things they tried to change and couldn't. Some things changed anyway. There was a core, something that made them, something that stayed the same. Some kind of continuity.

Knowledge had a danger out of all proportion to its size.
To entertain the possibility of never meaning anything, the
    boy oils his pistol,
poetry by any other name, naming and separating, moving
    away or toward.

From a certain distance, blue and round and singular, raid-ing empty lands, it wasn't everything and then it wasn't any-thing, walking a knife edge, leaving speech, to be only its passageway.

Sacrificing to the word. One must be called something.

Riding in the mountains with his eyes closed. He would dis-appear for several days.

In the backyard, broken bottles, rusted gaskets, hair curlers, a child's shirt, a man's dress shoe, some quarters, pieces of a metal shopping cart used for a barbecue.

A picket fence weaving around the rosebushes, paint flaked off, wires rusted through, each picket points a different way, bristling island in the lawn.

Where the days broke like confetti, bits that drifted to the streets below, the broad-shouldered industrialist waving to the crowds, fur collar catching paper specks, the cold air gray, overcoat gray, confetti gray.

This boy standing on the roof—his heart beat faster as he swept the snow, her hands grew colder as she called for him outside.

A broken-handled wagon and its rusty wheels—

or what else he'd done that day, fighting with his sisters over breakfast, building a snow fort in the neighbors' yard, tuning the radio.

The ones who made this history. This memory or history, my own eyes watching me.

———————

The same one who liked rabbits, elephants, and cars, in a warm snowsuit, age two.

Did not remember summer snowflakes, daylight stars, a cloud that drifted for the rest of time.

Before it happened, power lines, four lanes of cars, front lawns, driveways, a store—

ski jacket, age fourteen, tuxedo, age twenty-two.

———————

The origin of anything was startling—a plastic basket or a jar of jelly made nearby, some handsome wooden furniture —whimsy but not history;

no one explained streetlights that buzzed continually, insects in the silver cone like the intruders there, brown complicated things.

How to skin and butcher a rabbit.

This is one way to get the meat and hide from a rabbit you have killed.

Pierce the skin between the two hind legs, just in front of the anus. It helps if you pinch the skin between your fingers and lift it up a little. Try not to cut into the abdominal cavity, and you will save yourself a lot of mess.

Cut a slit all the way up to the chest. Push your fingers between the skin and muscle, and start pulling the skin away from the body.

Continue cutting the skin down the underside of each leg. Cut the feet off at the ankle. You also have to cut the anus away from the body.

Pull the hide off, cutting it when you get to the neck. Now cut the legs and shoulders off. Cut around where they join the body, then pull them out of the sockets to remove them.

Don't forget the tenderloins. This is the muscle on either side of the spine. It's more tender if you can remove the silvery sinew layer that covers the muscle.

That's about all the meat that's worth saving. Rinse all the hair and blood off in some water, then place all the meat in a bowl of clean water. Keep this in the fridge until you are ready to cook it.

If you want to save the hide, spread it out fur-side down and let it dry. Rabbit hides are very thin and tear easily. But they can last for years if you keep them dry.

In a white car, with a girl who was barely his wife.

There was some blurring at the edges, coming home and having dinner and a living room, a telephone, a clock. Her legs in seamless nylons, curled beneath her on the couch, a cocktail glass in hand. Clock ticking in the empty living room, the whole room—fireplace, walls, ceiling—painted white.

These men are rumpled. They feel deeply. They love their children and they want their children to do well. They want their children to be safe, and happy.

They are humble in their feeling. They believe their power is a public trust, a quantity they have been entrusted with. They are pilots of their own intelligence. They know they must appreciate it. They must act responsibly.

Each man performs investigations to convince himself his acts will be borne out by history.

Hers was a wall of photographs, of children who had lived there and grown up and gone.

This is a story about anything. About a family unfit for story-telling. I started over with it when I came. That may be hard to justify, talking about the past the way people talk about their own experiences. Everything happened the way I imagined it. Everything happened to me.

Threaded down a canyon barely visible, steep rivulet after a
rain, his knees pressed against the withers, reins gathered in
his hands, through sage brush, gravel, sand, a tangled mane,
a glistening hide, through terraced canyon walls toward un-
expected green,

sunrise at his back was pure white through his skin, bleached
trees white and sky white and white sand, he couldn't see it
but he felt light in the air,

who didn't know where he was going, didn't think that he
was going far, believed that everywhere he went the place he
left would stay the same, left at a walking pace and just kept
on,

ranch houses with no ranchers left in them,
ice in cocktail glasses and the cocktails gone.

Replace the story with itself, never static, squared, a flat field
by itself. The cat is gone, and how he stretched, ate, climbed,
jumped, ran, and how he cleaned himself.

89

The end of every party, napkins, toothpicks, glasses, empty trays.

War is that density of memory—collar of an overcoat, a conversation witnessed and recorded from behind the trees.

———————————

What is nostalgia when the past is always fiction?

———————————

When the sunset wasn't what we had expected. We defended space that took on meaning, was not simply ours, was what we were.

Green suns dropped below the fizzing line and Mrs. Oppenheimer knew that they would not come back.

With olives sinking, she fell off the path.

She couldn't hear. Unless she knew, there would have been no way.

They coded information in the private house chores of her day. Clean sheets. She might imagine that the house shook, or the house might really shake, a quick lurch that left one wondering. She might know everything, when it was done, in what order and for what reason, might know the accidents and failures and lucky breaks that went into the ultimate success.

In her sweater, skirt, and slim legs she still knew the trails, could camp with saddle bags and a bedroll.

This little boy as slender as a gun, most of him blew away before he could blow up inside.

A grandmother, or a picture of a grandmother, the baby's eyes the same soft blue, rabbits flushed young from the garden.

Swallowed in a flash of light, light burned through his summer shirt down to his shoulder blades, why heroes are impossible, he watched his father peeing on a rock.

From inside, watching at the door. First maple leaves seen through the screen.

Lost in the flood of photographs, a striped t-shirt, a calf led on a leash, a cardboard pen, a girl on roller skates, two sisters at the door, they peered outside while someone took a photograph, her hands red from the cold.

This one clean gun that should contain it all.

Newborns in the garden. Naked with their eyes still shut.

Children sewing stitches, needle finger jumping like the eye, to tell light how to travel in a sea where only some can be on top. Children pointing make a different face each time.

Nature, which in all its forms, always against us, knows no meaning. Knows nothing. Is mindless. Inhuman. Every beauty that we see is our projection.

92

Nature was only holding out a hand and we reached for it, nothing we could do could be outside of it,

absolutely inhuman now included one less thing, this new thing we could do that added one more entry to our column and took one of theirs away. It wasn't us that made it happen but we made it possible.

We could reverse the sequence if there'd ever been one, if it weren't that where we are is only ever part of where we are, pieces fit together only when they've come apart, paper crowding out the light, faces that once lay against each other where no seam had been.

After something blows apart, its wholeness is a fiction you construct. Pick any piece—the wholeness that it comes from comes from you.

The whole is something outside everything. It has no entry point. It won't break down. The past is only in relation to what isn't over yet.

We watched the pieces go to pieces. Scraps of paper that he dropped to calculate the power of the blast. We used simple instruments to measure what we'd done.

Then forever after we forgot that it was possible. We knew but then we didn't. This column that no one had ever seen before, it contained everything. And there were windows.

Blinking while the finger thinks of where to go. Rolling through the rhythm of the eye.

White ceiling and white walls and white-washed brick-front fireplace did not recede, ice didn't tinkle and the olives didn't stir. The air got whiter so it wasn't air, it was pure light but with an afterlife, the sun went up, blew up, came down, it broke apart and drifted out to sea. It was found everywhere. In pieces and around the world. It was as big as it could be.

"Get up," she said.

The point of the imagined is to put ourselves in places where we couldn't really be. On the back of a horse, at the edge of a blast. Riding away from the parents, who are already old. This girl's secret boyhood started in a world she didn't know but learned about. This girl wanted horses, and a boyhood, that would take her far from home.

"Get up."

Bibliography

Baudrillard, Jean. "L'Esprit Tu Terroisme." *Harper's* 304, no. 1821 (2002): 13.

Cohen, Daniel. *The Manhattan Project*. Brookfield, CT: The Mill-brook Press, 1999.

DeLano, Sharon. "The Torch Singer." *New Yorker* 78, no. 3 (2002): 48.

Derrida, Jacques. "Edmund Jabès and the Question of the Book." *A Book of the Book,* eds. Jerome Rothenberg and Steven Clay. New York: Granary, 2000.

Frascina, Francis, ed. *Pollack and After: The Critical Debate*. New York: Routledge, 2000.

Goodchild, Peter. *J. Robert Oppenheimer: Shatterer of Worlds*. New York: Fromm International, 1995.

Hersey, John. *Hiroshima*. New York: Alfred A. Knopf, 1985.

Leja, Michael. *Reframing Abstract Expressionism: Subjectivity and Painting in the 1940s*. New Haven: Yale University Press, 1993.

Moss, Norman. *The Politics of Uranium*. New York: Universe Books, 1982.

Rouze, Michel. *Robert Oppenheimer: The Man and His Theories*. Translated from the French by Patrick Evans. New York: Paul S. Eriksson, Inc., 1965.

Royal, Denise. *The Story of J. Robert Oppenheimer*. New York: St. Martin's Press, 1969.

Selden, Kyoko, and Mark Selden, eds. *The Atomic Bomb: Voices from Hiroshima and Nagasaki*. Armonk, NY: M. E. Sharpe, 1989.

Shohno, Naomi. *The Legacy of Hiroshima: Its Past, Our Future*. Tokyo: Kosei Publishing Co., 1986.

Smith, Richard Candida. *Utopia and Dissent: Art, Poetry, and Politics in California*. Berkeley: University of California Press, 1995.

Szasz, Ferenc Morton. *The Day the Sun Rose Twice*. Albuquerque: University of New Mexico Press, 1984.

Takaki, Ronald. *Hiroshima*. New York: Little, Brown, 1995.

Thomas, Gordon, and Max Morgan Witts. *Enola Gay*. New York: Stein and Day, 1977.

About the Author

Mary Burger was born in Ohio, the youngest of seven children whose births spanned the years from Hitler's invasion of Austria to Kennedy's assassination. She is the author of four previous works of poetry and prose: *Bleeding Optimist*, *Nature's Maw Gives and Gives*, *Thin Straw That I Suck Life Through*, and *The Boy Who Could Fly*. Since 1998 she has edited Second Story Books, featuring short works of experimental narrative. She is also co-editor of the online journal *Narrativity* and of *Biting the Error: Writers Explore Narrative*, an anthology of *Narrativity* contributors. She lives in California.

Leon Works

is an imprint of the L PROJECTS: PRESSES FOR NEW LITERATURE.
Renee Gladman, editor and publisher; Melissa Buzzeo, associate editor;
Rachel Bernstein, proofreader.

Leon extends special thanks to the following people whose contribu-
tions made this publication possible: Stefani Barber, Rachel Bernstein,
Jen Bervin, Anselm Berrigan and Karen Weiser, Taylor Brady and Tanya
Hollis, Poppy Brandes, Rebecca Brown, Norma Cole, Brenda Coultas,
Aja Duncan, Danielle Dutton and Martin Riker, Marcella Durand,
Laura Elrick, Brian Evenson, Thalia Field, Robert Fitterman, Tonya
Foster, Forrest Gander and C. D. Wright, Susan Gevirtz, Peter Gizzi,
Gwendolyn Gladman, Harriette Gladman, Vanessa Gladman, E. Tracy
Grinnell, Christina Hanhardt, Carla Harryman, Christian Hawkey,
Alex Hidalgo and Nate Bowler, Jen Hofer, Fanny Howe, Brenda Iijima,
Bhanu Kapil, Rosamond King, Aaron Kunin, Miranda Mellis, Emily
Eliot Miller, Tara Mulay, Eileen Myles, Travis Ortiz, Caitlin Parker,
Marjorie Perloff, Martha Reid, Leslie Scalapino, Gail Scott, Juliana
Spahr, Chuck Stebleton, Stacy Szymaszek, Roberto Tejada, Lynne Till-
man, Edwin Torres, Cathy Wagner, and Anne Waldman. And deepest
gratitude to Kenneth and Frances Reid, Rachel Levitsky, Mei-mei
Berssenbrugge, IC, and Jeff Clark for the extraordinary.